D0965869

■ この絵本の楽しみかた

● 日本文と英文のいずれでも物語を楽しめます。

● 英文は和文に基づいて詩のように書かれています。巻末 Notes を参考にして素晴らしい英詩文を楽しんでください。

● この「日本昔ばなし」の絵はかっての人気絵本「講談社の絵本」全203巻の中から厳選されたものです。

■ About this book

● The story is bilingual, written in both English and Japanese.

● The English is not a direct translation of the Japanese, but rather a retelling of the same story in verse form. Enjoy the English on its own, using the helpful Notes at the back.

● The illustrations are selected from volume 203 of the *Kodansha no ehon* (Kodansha Picture Books) series.

Distributed in the United States by Kodansha America, LLC, and in the United Kingdom and continental Europe by Kodansha Europe Ltd.

Published by Kodansha International Ltd., 17–14 Otowa 1-chome, Bunkyo-ku, Tokyo 112–8652.

ISBN 978–4–7700–2102–1
LCC 94–46336

First edition, 1995
Small-format edition, 1996

10th printing
Dai Nippon Printing Co., Ltd.
Tokyo, Japan
August 26, 2010

www.kodansha-intl.com

和英
併記

日本昔ばなし

きんたろう

KINTARO, THE NATURE BOY

え●よない すいほう

Illustrations by **Suiho Yonai**
Retold by **Ralph F. McCarthy**

KODANSHA INTERNATIONAL
Tokyo · New York · London

As Kintaro, the Nature Boy,
was chopping down a tree,
A bear jumped out and roared: "Begone!
These woods belong to me!"

むかしむかし，　あしがらやまの　きんたろうが
きを　きりたおして　いると，
くまが　おそいかかって　きました。

5

The lad just laughed and dropped his axe
to wrestle with the bear,
Then lifted it above his head
and spun it in the air.

それでも　きんたろうは　あわてず、
「えいっ。」と　くまを　もちあげると
「やっ。」と　なげすてて　しまいました。

6

The animals
 were all amazed
  and fell down at
   his feet.
"How strong he is!"
 they cried. "And yet,
  how gentle, kind,
   and sweet."

きんたろうは
その　ひから、
どうぶつたちの
たいしょうに
なりました。

9

From that day on,
    they came each day
    to visit Kintaro,
Whose mother taught
    him all the things
    a growing boy
    should know.

きんたろうは
りっぱな　ぶしに
なる　ために
おかあさんから　まいにち
べんきょうを　おそわりました。

And once he'd learned
his lessons well,
she gladly let him play.
She even made
a picnic lunch
for all of them one day.

ある　ひ,
きんたろうと　どうぶつたちは
おかあさんに　おむすびを
つくって　もらって,
やまおくに　あそびに
いく　ことに　しました。

The bear gave Kintaro a ride
and guided everyone
Along a path into the woods
for food and games and fun.

きんたろうは
くまの　せなかに　またがり,
しかは　おむすびを　せおい,
さるは　きの　はの
ぐんばいを　かついで,
やまみちを　のぼりました。

14

They made a ring of fallen leaves
beneath the sky of blue,
And there the creatures wrestled with
each other, two by two.

「さあ，　ここで　すもうを　とろう。」
きの　はを　あつめて
どひょうを　つくりました。
はっけよいよい　のこった
はっけよいよい　のこった
みんなで　ちからいっぱい
すもうを　とりました。

The monkey was the champ that day
of animal sumo,
But all of them together were
no match for Kintaro.

きんたろうに　くま　さる　しか　うさぎが
ちからを　あわせて　くみつきました。
「やー。」　きあいを　いれて,
きんたろうが　からだを
ゆすると,　どうぶつたちは
ころがされて　しまいました。

That evening, when
    they headed home,
    they found
    the bridge
    was gone,
But Kintaro
    knocked down
    a tree
    for them
    to cross
    upon.

かえりに
はしの　ない
たにに　さしかかると,
きんたろうは
たいぼくを　たおして,
みごとな　はしに
して　しまいました。

21

Now, watching from
the shadows with
a sparkle in his eye
Was Minamoto Raiko,
quite a famous
samurai.
Lord Raiko had
a soldier go
and ask this
strong young man
To join his band of warriors
—the bravest in Japan.

この　ようすを　みて　いた
ひとが　いました。
にっぽんいち
つよい　たいしょう，
みなもとの
らいこうです。

"Go with him, son," his mother said.
"It fills my heart with pride.
I wish your father could have seen
this day before he died."

きんたろうを　すっかり　きに　いって　しまった
みなもとの　らいこうは,
「ぜひ,　わたしの　けらいに　なって　ほしい。」
と,　おかあさんに　もうしいれました。
おかあさんは　この　もうしいれを
たいへん　よろこびました。

There was no greater honor than
to win Lord Raiko's praise,
And so his mother sent him off
to learn a soldier's ways.

そして　きんたろうは
みなもとの　らいこうの
けらいに　なりました。
なまえも　さかたの　きんときと
あらためました。

The boy bid all
his friends
farewell
and told them
not to cry.
"Next time we meet,"
he said,
"I'll be
a famous
samurai."

きんときは
おかあさんや
どうぶつたちと
わかれて,
みやこに　いく
ことに
なりました。

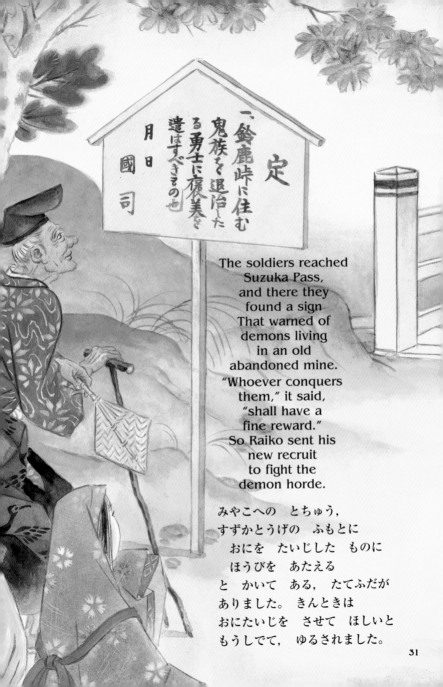

定

一、鈴鹿峠に住む
鬼族を退治した
る勇士に褒美を
遣はすべきもの也

月　日

國
司

The soldiers reached
Suzuka Pass,
and there they
found a sign
That warned of
demons living
in an old
abandoned mine.
"Whoever conquers
them," it said,
"shall have a
fine reward."
So Raiko sent his
new recruit
to fight the
demon horde.

みやこへの　とちゅう,
すずかとうげの　ふもとに
　おにを　たいじした　ものに
　ほうびを　あたえる
と　かいて　ある,　たてふだが
ありました。　きんときは
おにたいじを　させて　ほしいと
もうしでて,　ゆるされました。

たった　ひとりで
おにの　いわやに
のりこんだ　きんときは,
「わたしは　きんときと　いう,
　うたと　おどりの　じょうずな
　あかおにの　こどもだ。」
と　いって,　なかまに
もぐりこみました。

The boy ran up
　　the rocky path
　　as fast as he
　　could go,
And pounded on
　　the demons'
　　door.
　　"Who's that?"
　　"It's Kintaro!
I'm just a little
　　demon child
　　who loves to
　　dance and
　　sing.
Please let
　　me in to
　　entertain
　　His Majesty,
　　the King."

いわやの　なかで
さかもりを　して　いた
おにの　おやぶんは,
きんときが　じょうずに
おどるので　おおよろこびです。

The demon king was drinking wine,
    and glad to have the chance
To watch this little boy do such
    a fascinating dance.
And as our hero waved his axe
    and sang a funny song,
Applause and laughter filled the air—
    but not for very long.

35

For suddenly the boy began
to swing his axe around,
And six or seven demons fell,
beheaded, to the ground.
The others grabbed their iron clubs
and ran to crush their foe,
But all of them together were
no match for Kintaro.

ゆだんを　させて　おいて
きんときは　とつぜん
おにたちに　おそいかかり，
つぎつぎに　うちたおしました。
おにたちは　かなぼうを
ふりまわしましたが，　きんときの
つよさには　かないません。

37

He tied the king up with a rope
and led him through the town,
And all the people cheered the boy
who'd put the demons down.

ついに　きんときは、
おにの　おやぶんを
しばりあげて
しまいました。

39

"Well done, well done!" Lord Raiko said.
"I knew you'd prove your worth!
It seems to me that you must be
the strongest boy on earth!"

40

きんときが　たった　ひとりで
おにたいじを　した　ことを
しり，らいこうは
「さかたの　きんとき，よくぞ　やった。」
と，ほめました。

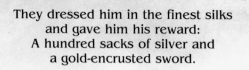

They dressed him in the finest silks
and gave him his reward:
A hundred sacks of silver and
a gold-encrusted sword.

らいこうは　ごほうびの　かたなを
きんときに　あたえ，　やくそくどおり
りっぱな　ぶしに　とりたてました。

His friends all came to celebrate
when Kintaro returned
Astride a stallion, bearing all
the treasures he had earned.

あしがらやまの　きんたろうは

しゅっせして，　おかあさんと
どうぶつたちの　まって　いる
やまおくに　かえって　きました。

おかあさんは りっぱな わがこの すがたを みて,
うれしさで むねが いっぱいに なりました。

"You've made me proud," his mother said. "My son, I love you so!" Which was, of course, the best reward of all for Kintaro.

Notes   きんたろう ◆Kintaro, the Nature Boy◆

p.5	roared ほえた Begone! 消えうせろ belong to ~ ～のものだ
p.6	laughed 笑った axe おの spun it in the air クマを空中でぐるぐるまわした
p.9	were all amazed 皆びっくりした fell down at his feet 彼の足元にひれふした
p.10	all the things a growing boy should know 成長期の子供が知るべきことをすべて
p.13	once he'd learned his lessons well 金太郎が勉強をちゃんと習い終わると
	gladly let him play 遊ぶのをよろこんで許してくれた
	even made a picnic lunch for all of them 全員にピクニックのお弁当さえ作ってくれた
p.14	gave Kintaro a ride 金太郎を乗せた along a path into the woods 森の奥への道を
	for food and games and fun 食べ物と遊びと楽しみを求めて
p.16	a ring of fallen leaves 落ち葉の土俵 creatures 生き物 two by two 2人ずつ
p.18	champ 優勝者 together were no match for ~ ～には全員でもかなわなかった
p.20	was gone なくなっていた for them to cross upon 彼らが渡れるように
p.23	with a sparkle in his eye 目を輝かせて had a soldier go 兵士を行かせた
	ask ~ to join his band of warriors ～に武士団に加わるよう頼む
p.24	It fills my heart with pride おまえが頼光殿と行くことは私の心を誇りで満たす I wish your
	father could have seen this day おまえの父がこの日を見ることができたらよかったのに
p.27	There was no greater honor than to win Lord Raiko's praise 頼光殿のおほめを勝ち取る
	ほど大きな名誉はなかった sent him off 彼を送り出した
p.28	bid all his friends farewell 友達みなに別れを告げた
p.31	a sign that warned of demons living in ~ ～に住んでいる鬼のことを警告する立て札
	abandoned mine 廃鉱 Whoever conquers them 鬼を征服する者はだれでも
	shall have a fine reward すばらしいほうびをもらうべし new recruit 新兵 horde 群れ
p.32	as fast as he could go できるだけ早く pounded たたいた
	Please let me in to entertain His Majesty 王様を楽しませるために入れてください
p.35	fascinating 魅力的な waved 揺らせた applause and laughter 拍手と笑い
	but not for very long それもあまり長くかんなかった
p.37	For というのも swing ~ around ～をふりまわす beheaded 首をはねられて
	to the ground 地面に grabbed つかんだ crush their foe 敵をやっつける
	together were no match for ~ ～には全員でもかなわなかった
p.39	tied ~ up with a rope ～を縛り上げた cheered ~ ～にかっさいした put ~ down ～を倒した
p.41	Well done よくやった I knew you'd prove your worth! おまえが自分の力を証明すると私に
	はわかっていた must be ~ ～にちがいない
p.42	the finest silks 最高の絹 reward ほうび A hundred sacks of ~ 百袋の～
	gold-encrusted sword 金細工された剣
p.44	Astride a stallion 立派な馬に乗って bearing all the treasures 宝物をもって
p.47	You've made me proud あなたのおかげで誇らしい気持です
	which was, of course, the best reward of all for Kintaro もちろんその言葉が金太郎には
	何よりも一番のごほうびでした (佐藤公俊)

和英併記 講談社バイリンガル絵本 日本昔ばなし きんたろう

1996年9月27日 第 1 刷発行	電話 03-3944-6493（編集部）
2010年8月26日 第10刷発行	03-3944-6492（マーケティング部・業務部）
	ホームページ www.kodansha-intl.com

絵	米内穂豊	印刷・製本所 大日本印刷株式会社
訳 者	ラルフ・マッカーシー	
協 力	講談社児童局	落丁本・乱丁本は購入書店名を明記のうえ、小社業務部宛にお送りください。送料小社
発行者	廣田浩二	負担にてお取替えします。なお、この本についてのお問い合わせは、編集部宛にお願い
発行所	講談社インターナショナル株式会社	いたします。本書の無断複写（コピー）、転載は著作権法の例外を除き、禁じられています。
	〒112-8652 東京都文京区音羽1-17-14	© 講談社インターナショナル株式会社 1995 Printed in Japan
		ISBN 978-4-7700-2102-1